Happy Ever After

Books sh
above. Re
www.kent.g

_____

_____

Libraries &

For Cerys
S.W.

ORCHARD BOOKS
338 Euston Road, London NW1 3BH
Orchard Books Australia
Level 17/207 Kent Street, Sydney, NSW 2000

First published in hardback in 2010 by Orchard Books
First published in paperback in 2011

ISBN 978 1 40830 751 9 (HB)
ISBN 978 1 40830 757 1 (PB)

Text © Tony Bradman 2010
Illustrations © Sarah Warburton 2010

A CIP catalogue record for this book is available from the British Library.

1 3 5 7 9 10 8 6 4 2 (HB)
1 3 5 7 9 10 8 6 4 2 (PB)

Printed in Great Britain

Orchard Books is a division of Hachette Children's Books,
an Hachette UK company.
www.hachette.co.uk

Tony Bradman

Happy Ever After

Illustrated by Sarah Warburton

ORCHARD BOOKS

It was a lovely morning, and the sun shone on Mr Giant as he walked into the village to do his weekly shopping. He was careful where he put his boots, of course. But he needn't have worried. The villagers weren't scared – they were pleased to see him.

"Hey there, Mr Giant!" people called out happily. "How are things?"

"Er…couldn't be better, thanks," said Mr Giant with a shy smile.

In fact, he could hardly believe how well things were going for him these days. He still had occasional nightmares about Jack, and hoped he would never, ever meet him again.

But he was also grateful to the little rascal – Jack had made him think about the kind of life he was living.

The truth was that up there in his castle,
Mr Giant had been rather bored and lonely.
He'd had no hobbies or interests, and no friends.
Everybody had always run off screaming
as soon as they heard him start to growl,
"Fee, fi, fo, fum..."

A week in the Fairy Tale Clinic For
Recovering Villains had made all the difference.
He had learnt that he could change if he wanted
to, and Mr Giant had promised himself he would
give up being nasty and violent…for ever.

He decided to leave his castle, and moved
to a lovely village on the far side of the Forest.
Mr Giant settled down to live a peaceful,
happy life. The villagers were nice to him right
from the start, and he soon made plenty of friends.

He joined the Village Social Club...

...and took up stamp collecting.

Now the only problems he had were small ones. His cottage was a bit cramped, and he didn't think he would ever get used to eating such tiny portions of food...

Today Mr Giant soon finished his shopping and set off for home. But suddenly he heard shouting, and went back to find out what was happening. He stopped behind an enormous old oak tree and peered out.

A short, plump man with a mean face was standing on one of the benches outside the village tavern. He was shouting at a group of villagers, who were being pushed around by a band of tough-looking soldiers.

"I'm Baron Beastly, your new lord and master," the short man yelled. "And I'm doubling… no, *tripling* your taxes. You have till next week to pay me.'

"What if we can't?" said somebody. "We don't have that much money."

"You'd better find it, then," snapped
Baron Beastly, glaring at the villagers.
"Otherwise I'll get my soldiers to burn down
your pretty little village.

"And don't think I won't do it, either.
I'm beastly by nature as well as by name…"

Mr Giant felt anger boiling up inside him as he listened. "Fee, fi, fo, fum…" he murmured.

Now Baron Beastly and his beastly men were marching out of the village, and Mr Giant almost followed them. He had a vision of just what he would do.

Then Mr Giant realised what he was
thinking, and felt ashamed. He had made
a promise not to be like that, and he was
determined not to break it.

Once he started behaving badly, he was
worried he wouldn't be able to stop.

That evening, the villagers held a crisis meeting in the village hall. Mr Giant squeezed in with everybody else, and listened to them argue about what to do.

"We need somebody who can stand up to Baron Beastly," said one of the villagers eventually. "Somebody who could really scare the pants off him."

"What about you, Mr Giant?" said the
village baker. "You're a big lad. I bet you could
be pretty scary if you put your mind to it."

"No, count me out. I don't do that kind of thing," muttered Mr Giant. He could feel everybody staring at him, and he blushed.

"Oh, right, er…fair enough," said the baker, raising his eyebrows. A sigh of disappointment rustled through the hall. "It'll have to be Plan B, then."

Plan B was simple. The villagers put together
all the money they had, even their savings
and the coins from their children's piggy banks.

That wasn't enough, so they sold
their jewellery...

...and even their best animals.

Mr Giant chipped in with everything he had, too. He wondered if the villagers were annoyed with him. But they seemed very thankful for his money, and were just as nice to him as ever...

...which made him feel all the more guilty, of course.

"It looks like we've hit the target," said
the baker. "We'll give the money to Baron Beastly
tomorrow and our troubles will be over."

Their troubles weren't over, though. Early the next day, Baron Beastly marched into the village with his men. He shouted at the villagers, demanding the money, and they handed it over.

Baron Beastly laughed, and did
a little victory dance.

"There you go, that wasn't hard, was it?"
he said with a smirk. "And seeing as you're so
good at raising money, I'll be back next week for
the same again."

"*Next week?!*" squeaked the baker.

The crowd behind him groaned.

"We won't be able to come up with a penny more.
The village is totally broke."

"Well, that's not *my* problem," said Baron
Beastly, shrugging. "Either you find the cash,
or you'll be homeless this winter. It's up to you…"

The villagers held another crisis meeting that afternoon, but nobody could think of a solution.

Mr Giant listened to them arguing, then sadly trudged back to his little cottage.

He sat alone, his colossal head in his huge hands.

His mind was in a whirl. He wanted to help his friends and save the village, but he couldn't break his promise. It was all too difficult to think about. Only somebody really clever would be able to work out what he should do.

Then suddenly it hit him. He knew exactly the right person – although the thought of meeting Jack again sent shivers of fear down his spine. But he would have to do it if he wanted to save the village.

So Mr Giant wrote a letter.

A couple of days later there was a
knock-knock on Mr Giant's door.

"Hey there, big guy!" said Jack. "Great to see
you! How are things?"

"Not so good, actually," murmured Mr Giant. "I, er...need your help."

A nervous Mr Giant invited Jack in...

...and they talked over tea and cakes.

"What are you worried about?" said Jack at last. "You should just put the frighteners on this Baron Beastly creep, then carry on being the new you."

"But do you think I can do both?" said Mr Giant. "What if I can't control myself? What if I slip back into my old ways and start being nasty again?"

"You can do anything if you set your mind to it," said Jack. "That's how a little guy like me managed to run rings round a big guy like you, anyway."

"Really?" said Mr Giant, offering him more cake. "I see what you mean…"

So a week later, when Baron Beastly and his men marched into the village to collect the taxes, they got a nasty surprise.

A colossal shadow fell over them and Mr Giant put on his scariest face.

He **ROARED**,

and **STAMPED**

his massive great boots…

...and his huge voiced boomed out,

"Fee, fi, fo, fum! Look out Baron Beastly, here I come!"

Baron Beastly and his men ran screaming out of the village.

For a brief moment Mr Giant felt like following them to finish the job.

But he didn't. He thought of Jack instead, and kept himself firmly under control.

Baron Beastly and his men never, ever returned to the village. In fact, the baron was so terrified of Mr Giant, he sent all the villagers' money back. And to thank his friend, the baker made Mr Giant an absolutely *ENORMOUS* cake.

So, against all the odds, the villagers
and Mr Giant managed to live...
HAPPILY EVER AFTER!

Also by Tony Bradman

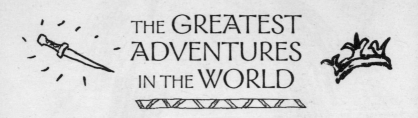

THE GREATEST
ADVENTURES
IN THE WORLD

TONY BRADMAN & TONY ROSS

Jason and the Voyage to the Edge of the World	978 1 84362 472 1
Arthur and the King's Sword	978 1 84362 475 2
Aladdin and the Fabulous Genie	978 1 84362 477 6
Ali Baba and the Stolen Treasure	978 1 84362 473 8
Robin Hood and the Silver Arrow	978 1 84362 474 5
William Tell and the Apple for Freedom	978 1 84362 476 9
Robinson Crusoe, Shipwrecked	978 1 84362 572 0
Beowulf the Hero	978 1 84362 574 4
Gulliver in Lilliput	978 1 84362 576 8
David and Goliath	978 1 84362 578 2

All priced at £3.99

Orchard books are available from all good bookshops,
or can be ordered from our website: www.orchardbooks.co.uk,
or telephone 01235 827702, or fax 01235 827703

Prices and availability are subject to change.